This Little Tiger
book belongs to:

_____

_____

_____

For Tony, with love
_MCB

For Ella + Alan
_TM

LITTLE TIGER PRESS
An imprint of Magi Publications
1 The Coda Centre, 189 Munster Road, London SW6 6AW
www.littletigerpress.com

First published in Great Britain 2004
This edition published 2006

Printed in China

2 4 6 8 10 9 7 5 3 1

One Snowy Night

M Christina Butler

illustrated by Tina Macnaughton

LITTLE TIGER PRESS
London

The cold wind woke Little Hedgehog
from his deep winter sleep. It blew his
blanket of leaves high into the air,
and he shivered in the snow. He tried
to sleep again, but he was far too cold.

Suddenly, something fell from the sky . . .

...BUMP!

It landed right in front of his nose.
It was a parcel, and it had his name on it.

To Little Hedgehog
With Love From
Father Christmas xx

Little Hedgehog opened the parcel as fast as he could. Inside was a red woolly bobble hat . . . hedgehog size!

He put it on at once.
He pulled it to the back.
He pulled it to the front.
He pulled it to one side,
then the other . . .

But no matter how he stretched it
to fit, his prickles got in the way *every time*.
By now the hat was far too big for a
little hedgehog.

He took it off and gazed at it,
until at last he had an idea . . .

He gave the hat a shake
and wrapped it up again.
He tore a bit off the label
and wrote on the rest.

Happy Christmas Rabbit
With love from
Little Hedgehog xxx

Then off he ran to Rabbit's house.
Rabbit was out, so he left the present
on his doorstep.

It was snowing hard as
Little Hedgehog tried to find his
way back home. The snowflakes flew
all around, and he wasn't sure which
way to go.

"Oh dear, oh dear," he said as he pattered
to and fro. "I shouldn't have come out
in this weather. But I'm sure Rabbit
will be pleased to have a nice
woolly hat to wear."

"Bother the snow!" said Rabbit,
rushing home. He spotted the parcel
lying on his doorstep.
   "What's this?" he squeaked with delight,
ripping off the paper. "A bobble hat,"
he cried. "For ME!"

He put it on at once. He tried it with
his ears inside, and then outside.
He pulled it this way and
he pulled it that way.
But no matter how
he stretched it to fit,
his ears got in
the way . . .
every time!

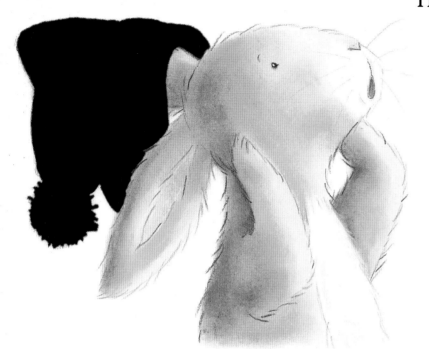

By now the hat was
very much bigger. It was
far too big for a rabbit.
So . . .

. . . Rabbit wrapped up the hat once again,
and wrote on a corner of the label.
Then off he went to Badger's house.

The cold weather made Badger very
grumpy.
  "Happy Christmas, Badger!"
shouted Rabbit.
  "Who's there?" growled Badger.
  "Happy Christmas!" repeated Rabbit,
giving him the parcel.

"A Christmas present?"
said Badger.
"For ME?"

Badger put the hat on.

He pulled it down over his ears.

"What . . . about . . . THAT!"

he said, looking in the mirror.

"Very nice," said Rabbit.

"What did you say?" said Badger.

"*Very nice!*" yelled Rabbit,

hopping off.

"Don't you like it?" asked
Badger, turning round.
But Rabbit had gone.
Badger took the hat off.
"This is no good to me,"
he said. "I can't hear
a thing. What a pity.
It's such a nice colour."

So Badger wrapped up
the parcel and marched
off to Fox's house.
He didn't bother
with a label.

Fox was going out exploring.

"Here you are, friend," said Badger merrily.

"A Christmas present, especially for you!"

"Christmas?" snapped Fox, puzzled.

"Yes, Christmas!" called Badger.

"Time to be nice to each other!"

And he plodded off.

"A hat?" sneered Fox, opening the parcel. "What do I want with a hat?"

Then he looked at the hat again . . .

He made two holes for his ears and put it on. Satisfied, he went on his way.

The white fields twinkled in the
moonlight. Fox sniffed around and
found a small trail. He followed it this way
and that way until suddenly it stopped.
There was something under the snow!

Fox began to dig and dig,
until he found a small hedgehog.
It was cold and did not move.
"Poor little fellow," said Fox.
He put the hedgehog inside the
red woolly hat and carried
it to Rabbit's house.

Rabbit and Badger were having supper.
  "Look what I've found in the snow!"
cried Fox, bursting in.
  They all looked into
the hat.

"A hedgehog?" said Badger.
"What's a hedgehog doing out at
Christmas time? He should be fast asleep!"
"It's my friend Little Hedgehog!" cried
Rabbit. "He must have got lost going
home in the snow!"
Little Hedgehog opened his eyes.
"Hello," he said sleepily. "Oh, this
is such a lovely warm blanket."

The friends all looked at each other.
Rabbit grinned and Fox scratched his head.
  "Hmmm," said Badger. "I think this woolly
hat is *just right* for Little Hedgehog!"
  "Happy Christmas, Little Hedgehog!"
they all cried . . . but Little Hedgehog
was fast asleep!

Little Tiger books – the perfect present every time!

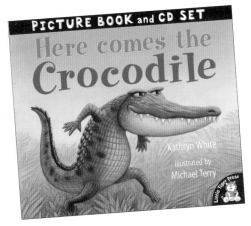

PICTURE BOOK and CD SET
Here comes the **Crocodile**
Kathryn White
Illustrated by Michael Terry

PICTURE BOOK and CD SET
Laura's Star
Klaus Baumgart

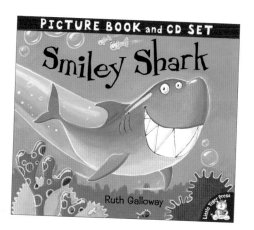

PICTURE BOOK and CD SET
Smiley Shark
Ruth Galloway

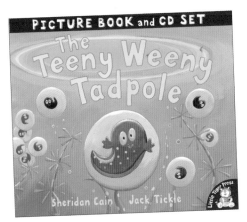

PICTURE BOOK and CD SET
The Teeny Weeny Tadpole
Sheridan Cain · Jack Tickle

PICTURE BOOK and CD SET
I don't want to go to bed!
Julie Sykes · Tim Warnes

For information regarding any of the above titles
or for our catalogue, please contact us:
Little Tiger Press, 1 The Coda Centre,
189 Munster Road, London SW6 6AW, UK
Tel: 020 7385 6333
Fax: 020 7385 7333
E-mail: info@littletiger.co.uk
www.littletigerpress.com